Do you have a dresser
with a stuck drawer?

-Grandpa Frank + Grandma Sandy
Dec., 1996

ONE STUCK DRAWER

LAURA NYMAN MONTENEGRO

Houghton Mifflin Company

Boston   1991

To my Parents and Andra,
Michael, Sonya, and Nina

Library of Congress Cataloging-in-Publication Data

Montenegro, Laura Nyman.
    One stuck drawer / Laura Nyman Montenegro.
        p.   cm.
    Summary: Visiting a furniture store, a young girl falls in love
with an old dresser, but can't pay for it until the dresser's stuck
drawer provides a solution.
    ISBN 0-395-57319-X
    [1. Furniture—Fiction.]   I. Title.
[E]—dc20PZ7.M76350n   1991   90-46139
                                   CIP
                                   AC

Printed in the United States of America

HOR 10 9 8 7 6 5 4 3 2 1

There once was a dresser with one stuck drawer.

For a long time the dresser sat in a used
furniture store, waiting to be sold.
But no one could open the dresser's bottom drawer.
"What good is a dresser with one stuck drawer?"
people would say. "It's useless."
And so it was moved down to the basement
of the store, where it would no longer be in the way.
The dresser hated the basement.
It was dark and clammy.

Sometimes at night the dresser had a dream.
It was a dream of happiness. But in the morning, the dresser
would wake to find itself in the same dreary basement.

Day after day, the dresser lived this way.
Then one morning, the door at the top of the stairs opened a tiny bit.
A girl peered down into the darkness. Her name was Sophia.

The storekeeper led her down the stairs to the dresser.
"Take a look," he grumbled, "Old One-Stuck-Drawer!
I'm only showing it to you because all of our nice dressers are gone.
Do you want it?"

"Oh yes!" said Sophia, "I love it! But I don't have enough money for it."
"Take it now," the storekeeper said. "You can pay me next week."
The movers lifted the dresser up out of the dark basement into the bright,
sunny street and carried it all the way to Sophia's house.

They put the dresser in Sophia's little room.
"Be sure to pay us by the end of the week," the movers warned.
"Maybe you'll be lucky and find a treasure in the bottom drawer.
It's stuck, you know!" The movers laughed.

Sophia fixed a special place for her new friend. She sang
songs and read stories to the dresser. It had never been so happy.
But there was one thing wrong — Sophia had no money.

Then one night it happened.

Sophia and the dresser woke to shouts and
the slamming of truck doors down in the street.
Sophia bolted to the window.

Under the streetlight sat
a big, empty moving van.

Sophia ran to the door and listened.

She heard the movers' shoes clumping up the stairs.

Up, up, up they came until they stopped — outside HER door!

They tumbled into the room.
"WE WANT THE DRESSER!"

"Please don't take it," Sophia cried.
The movers lifted the dresser high into the air.
"If you don't pay, we take it away!" they laughed.
Sophia threw her arms around the dresser
and held on with all her might.

But the dresser was sliding out of her arms. She clutched the knob
on the stuck drawer. The movers yanked the dresser away.
Shoof! The drawer opened. Out dropped a strange little bundle.

"Now, let's go," mumbled one of the movers.
Sophia fell to the floor, holding the bundle.

The dresser was frightened.
The big truck rolled back to the store.
As they set the dresser in the front window,
the movers said, "If it doesn't sell tomorrow,
we'll use it for firewood. It will make
excellent kindling."
The truck roared away.

As the dresser sat peering out the window
into the empty streets, it shivered.
"What a horrible thing, to be thrown into a FIRE,
to be no more than sticks and smoke
—oh, what a horrible thing. I wish Sophia was here."
Suddenly a figure appeared in the darkness.
"SOPHIA . . . ?"
No. It was not Sophia, only a passing stranger.

From where the dresser sat, it could see Sophia's
window at the top of a tall, sleeping building.
Her window was dark. Through the long night,
the dresser watched the window.
Finally a light appeared. "Ah," thought the dresser,
"Sophia must be opening the bundle."
And satisfied, the dresser fell wearily asleep.

In the morning a shout woke the dresser. "Oh, they're here, they're here," the dresser moaned. "The movers have come to get me." But looking out into the street, the dresser saw a crowd instead. Suddenly the crowd swayed. It parted. And in the middle . . .

DANCED AN EXTRAORDINARY TIGER!

It leaped . . .

It whirled . . .

It stalked . . .

It twirled . . .

And from the crowd came cheers and a shower of coins.
Bowing deeply, the tiger removed its beautiful mask. It was Sophia!

Sophia gathered the coins from the sidewalk
and ran to the window. She smiled at the dresser.
"Now I can take you home," she cried.
"See! See what I found! Magical cloth, and shoes,
and a beautiful mask! They were in your drawer.
The one that was stuck!
Your ONE STUCK DRAWER!"